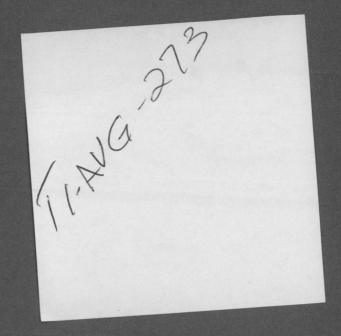

Chimpanzees for TEA!

by

Jo Empson

Philomel Books

"Hey, Vincent!
This cupboard is looking a bit bare.
Can you rush to the shops . . .

. . . and get:

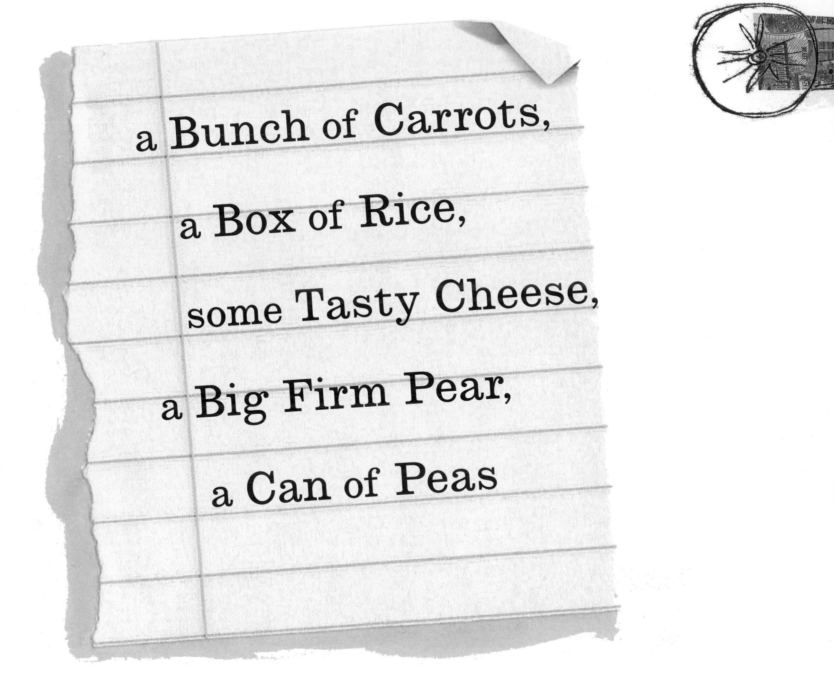

a Bunch of Carrots,

a Box of Rice,

some Tasty Cheese,

a Big Firm Pear,

a Can of Peas

and hurry home in time for tea!"

Sorry, can't stop, Mr. Singh.
I've got to rush to the shops and get . . .
a Bunch of Carrots, a Box of Rice,
some Tasty Cheese, a Big Firm Pear, a Can of Peas

and hurry home in time for tea.   BUT . . .

Oh
NO...
the

list!

What was it? Umm . . . a Bunch of Carrots . . . errr . . .

a Box of Rice, some Tasty Cheese . . . a Big Firm Pear . . .

...a **Trapeze** and hurry home in time for tea.

. . . I've got to rush to the shops and get a Bunch

of Carrots, a Box of Rice, some Tasty Cheese . . .

aaaa . . .

aaaa . . .

aaaand . . .

. . . a Big Furry Bear, a Trapeze

and hurry home

. . . some Chimpanzees, a Big Furry

Bear, a Trapeze . . .

and hurry home
in time for tea.

rush to the shops and get a Bunch of Carrots . . .

. . . a **Box of Mice**, some Chimpanzees, a Big Furry Bear, a Trapeze and hurry home in time for tea.

. . . a Branch of Parrots,
a Box of Mice, some Chimpanzees,

a Big Furry Bear, a Trapeze. Hurry home and . . .

. . . invite

them ALL in for . . .

...tea!

For John with love & thanks — J.E.

PHILOMEL BOOKS
an imprint of Penguin Random House LLC
375 Hudson Street, New York, NY 10014

Library of Congress Cataloging-in-Publication Data is available upon request.
Manufactured in China by RR Donnelley Asia Printing Solutions Ltd.
ISBN 978-1-101-99621-8
10 9 8 7 6 5 4 3 2 1

Text set in New Clarendon MT Std. The art was done in watercolor.